Hiya! My name Thudd. Best robot friend of Drewd. Thudd know lots of stuff. Why ocean is salty. How octopus change color. Why continents always moving.

Drewd like to invent stuff. Thudd help! Now Drewd help Uncle Al make new underwater invention. Oop! Accident happen! Adventure happen! Want to come along? Look for giant squid? Turn page, please!

Get lost with
Andrew, Judy, and Thudd
in all their exciting adventures!

Andrew Lost on the Dog
Andrew Lost in the Bathroom
Andrew Lost in the Kitchen
Andrew Lost in the Garden
Andrew Lost Under Water

AND COMING SOON!
Andrew Lost in the Whale

ANDREW LOST

5

UNDER WATER

BY J. C. GREENBURG

ILLUSTRATED
BY MIKE REED

A STEPPING STONE BOOK™

Random House 🏠 New York

www.randomhouse.com/kids
www.AndrewLost.com

Library of Congress Cataloging-in-Publication Data
Greenburg, J. C. (Judith C.)
Under water / by J. C. Greenburg ; illustrated by Mike Reed.
   p.   cm. — (Andrew Lost ; 5)
"A stepping stone book."
SUMMARY: Andrew, his cousin Judy, and Thudd the robot accidentally set off in Uncle Al's latest invention, a Volkswagen Beetle converted for deep-sea exploration, and try to prevent the evil Soggy Bob from taking a rare ocean creature.
ISBN 0-375-82523-1 (trade) — ISBN 0-375-92523-6 (lib. bdg.)
[1. Underwater exploration—Fiction. 2. Marine animals—Fiction.
3. Inventions—Fiction. 4. Cousins—Fiction.]   I. Reed, Mike, ill.
II. Title. III. Series: Greenburg, J. C. (Judith C.). Andrew lost ; 5.
PZ7.G82785 Un 2003   [Fic]—dc21   2002152100

Printed in the United States of America
First Edition 10 9 8

CONTENTS

ANDREW'S WORLD

Andrew Dubble

Andrew is ten years old, but he's been inventing things since he was four. Some of his inventions have gotten him into trouble, like the time he shrunk himself, his cousin Judy, and his little silver robot Thudd down to microscopic size.

Today Andrew is showing off his Uncle Al's newest invention, the Water Bug. It's an underwater vehicle made to explore the deepest ocean. What could possibly go wrong?

Judy Dubble

Judy is Andrew's thirteen-year-old cousin. She thought she was too smart to let Andrew drag her into another crazy adventure. But that was before he showed her the Water Bug. . . . Who knew she'd end up deep under the Pacific Ocean trying to save giant squids?

Thudd

The Handy Ultra-Digital Detective. Thudd is a super-smart robot and Andrew's best friend. Thudd must never get wet. If he does, his thought chips could get soggy. Perhaps a voyage to the deepest ocean isn't such a good idea. . . .

Uncle Al

Andrew and Judy's uncle is a top-secret scientist. He invented Thudd! Uncle Al can't stop working on his inventions, even when he's on vacation. But after today, he may wish he hadn't invented the Water Bug!

The Water Bug

It used to be an old Volkswagen Beetle until Uncle Al turned it into a submarine. Now it's got a glass floor, a sharky fin on its roof, and a bathroom in the backseat. And it wants to take Andrew, Judy, and Thudd to the deepest part of the ocean!

Soggy Bob Sloggins

This bad guy of the sea is building Animal Universe, the biggest theme park in the world. But he doesn't care about the animals. He's just hung a sign above the huge aquarium in Squid World. It says SOGGY BOB'S GIANT SQUIDWICHES—COMING SOON! Will Andrew, Judy, and Thudd be able to stop Soggy Bob from turning giant squids into snacks?

1 BYE-BYE, HAWAI'I!

Andrew Dubble looked up through the tall palm trees.

"This reminds me of when we were lost in the dog-hair forest on Harley's nose!" he said.

"*Eeeuw!*" said his cousin Judy. She gave a little shiver. "I don't *ever* want to think about that! Do you *have* to be so irritating on our last morning in Hawai'i?"

Judy tossed her frizzy hair and marched toward the ocean. She kicked up little fountains of sand with every step. Andrew followed her.

meep . . . "Drewd and Oody gotta pack now!" came a squeaky voice from Andrew's shirt pocket. It was Thudd, a little silver robot and Andrew's best friend. "Plane leave in three hours!"

"I guess you're right," sighed Judy. "But I just hate to leave."

Their trip to Hawai'i had been so much fun. They'd swum with dolphins, eaten seaweed salad, and taken an amazing helicopter ride over a volcano!

Andrew and Judy had been surprised when Judy's parents took them to Hawai'i after the mess they'd gotten into three weeks ago. That was when Andrew had accidentally shrunk himself, Judy, and Thudd to microscopic size with the Atom Sucker. They'd been snuffled into a dog's nose, flushed down a toilet, carried off by a cockroach, and dragged into an anthill!

Their parents had been a *little* upset. But

mostly, they were proud of the kids for solving the big problem of being very little.

"Before we finish packing," said Andrew, "there's something I've got to show you."

"What?" asked Judy.

"It's a surprise," said Andrew.

Judy looked at Andrew. Her eyes narrowed. "What kind of surprise?" she asked suspiciously. "The last time you surprised me, I ended up swimming in dog snot."

Andrew laughed. "It's a surprise for Uncle Al. He has this new invention. But he's been so busy taking us around Hawai'i, he hasn't had time to finish it. So I've been getting up early every morning to work on it. After breakfast, I'm going to show Uncle Al what I did."

"Cheese Louise!" said Judy. "You've been messing around with one of Uncle Al's inventions? He'll have a cow!"

Andrew shook his head. "Uh-uh," he

said. "Come on. We'll be back in ten minutes."

Judy rolled her eyes. "I'd better check this out before Uncle Al does," she said.

Andrew led the way down the beach. Huge blue waves were crashing onto the white sand.

"Wowzers!" said Andrew. "Look how high the waves are!"

meep . . . "High tide!" said Thudd. "Moon pull big lump of water to this side of earth! See?"

Thudd pointed to his face screen.

They came to a quiet lagoon surrounded by palm trees. A few small boats were anchored there.

Andrew walked up to a garage at the edge of the water. There was a small box in the middle of the door. Andrew talked into the box. "Good golly, Miss Molly," he said.

Chugga chugga chugga came a noise from inside the garage. The garage door rolled up slowly.

Andrew stepped inside and clicked on the light.

"Ta-da!"

HELLO, WATER BUG!

"It's the Water Bug!" said Andrew.

Judy's eyes got wide. "Cheese Louise!" she said.

A Volkswagen Beetle was parked on a ramp above the water. But this car wasn't like one you would see on the street.

This Beetle was a strange color that shifted from silver to red to blue. It had a sharky fin on its roof. It had fishy gills on its doors. And instead of rubber tires, the Water Bug had paddle wheels.

"The first day we got to Hawai'i," said

Andrew, "Uncle Al let me help him with the Water Bug."

"How come it's such a weird color?" asked Judy.

"It's got this coating called Protectum," said Andrew. "It can change color to disguise itself. It can even light up in the dark."

Andrew pointed to a silver nose on the front of the Water Bug. It looked like a hood ornament.

"This is the Super-Sniffer," said Andrew. "It tracks things like dogs do, by smell. Uncle Al made it, and I put it on."

"Bizarr-o!" said Judy.

Andrew opened the door on the passenger side. "Hop in," he said.

Judy folded her arms. "Are you kidding?" she said. "I'm not getting into anything *you* fooled around with."

"Jeepers creepers," said Andrew. "I just want to show you the inside."

Judy rolled her eyes. "Oh, all right," she said, plopping down in the passenger's seat. Andrew shut Judy's door, then walked around and got into the driver's seat.

The front seats of the Water Bug looked like the ones in a regular car. But the dashboard was crammed with dials and buttons. Next to the steering wheel was a microphone. There was a gas pedal and a brake on the floor—but the floor was made of glass!

The back of the Water Bug had been divided into two spaces. On one side was a tiny kitchen with a little refrigerator, a microwave oven, and a sink with a cabinet underneath. On the other side was the smallest bathroom ever.

Judy shook her head. "You could *live* in this thing," she said.

Andrew smiled. "And it even talks to you," he said.

Andrew reached for the biggest black dial

on the dashboard and turned it till it clicked.

glurp . . . "Welcome to the Water Bug!" said a mechanical voice. "Would you like to take a tour of the beach? Visit a coral reef? Explore the deepest ocean? Search for giant squids?"

"Um, nothing right now, thanks," said Andrew. He tried to turn the dial farther.

KRACK!

The dial fell onto the floor!

glurp . . . "Something is wrong with my destination dial," said the Water Bug. "Please repeat your choice."

"No ocean!" said Andrew. "No squids!"

glurp . . . "Thank you!" said the Water Bug. "You have chosen to explore the deepest ocean. To search for giant squids, please turn on the Super-Sniffer."

VROOOM!

The Water Bug's engine came to life!

Chugga chugga chugga . . .

The ramp tilted down, the door that led to the ocean rolled up, and the Water Bug slid into the water!

The paddle wheels started spinning, splashing water onto the windows. The Water Bug zoomed out of the garage and into the lagoon!

"Wowzers schnauzers!" said Andrew.

"Andrew!" yelled Judy. "We've got to go back!"

Andrew turned the steering wheel, but the Water Bug kept going straight.

"Um, I'm not sure I can go back," said Andrew.

"*WHAT?*" yelled Judy.

"Well, uh, when the destination dial got loose, I think the Water Bug got stuck on auto-pilot. It's steering itself now."

Judy picked the dial up off the floor and waved it in front of Andrew's nose.

"This dial isn't loose, bug-brain," she said. *"You broke it off!"*

The Water Bug zipped out of the peaceful blue lagoon into the choppy waves of the ocean.

Andrew could see the beach in his rearview mirror. The garage and the palm trees were getting smaller and smaller.

"ANDREW!" yelled Judy. "Get this thing back to the garage! *Now!"*

Andrew looked over the buttons on the dashboard and pressed a yellow one.

"I think Uncle Al said something about this one," he said.

"Noop! Noop! Noop!" squeaked Thudd.

But it was too late.

Sluuurp! came a sucking sound. The doors and windows sealed shut. The Water Bug tilted down and dove under the waves!

GOING DOWN!

"Yikes!" yelled Judy.

"Yowzers!" yelled Andrew.

"Yeep!" squeaked Thudd.

The Water Bug sped down and down. Slanted beams of sunlight lit up the blue-green world below.

A dial on the dashboard measured how deep they were. The meter said ten feet, then twenty feet, then thirty feet.

Judy shook her head. "Well, smarty-pants," she said. "You've gotten us into giant trouble again! The air in here won't last long."

meep . . . "Water Bug got gills on doors," said Thudd. "Pull oxygen from water same way fish do. Lotsa oxygen molecules in water."

"Good!" said Judy. "At least we'll be breathing when some gross sea monster turns us into a snack. Maybe it will be one of those giant squids! What *are* those things anyway?"

meep . . . "Giant squid strange, strange, strange!" said Thudd. "Cousin of octopus. Long as two school buses! Got eyes the size of dinner plates! No human ever seen giant squid alive. Look!"

Thudd pointed to his face screen.

"Wowzers schnauzers!" said Andrew. "It looks kind of interesting."

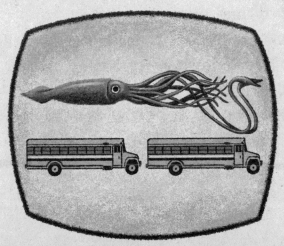

Judy rolled her eyes. "Oh brother!" she said. "Come on, guys. Let's figure out some way to get back. *Quick!*"

Andrew studied the buttons and dials. "Hmmm . . . ," he said.

Judy groaned. "'Hmmm' does not sound like someone who knows what he's doing."

meep . . . "Thudd call Uncle Al," said Thudd.

There were three rows of buttons on Thudd's chest. They all glowed green except for the big purple button in the middle. This was the one Thudd used to send emergency messages to Uncle Al.

Thudd pressed the big purple button. It blinked three times.

Colors flashed beneath the glass floor. Judy leaned down to see.

"Look at this!" she said.

Below the Water Bug swam schools of fish. Their colors weren't like the colors on land. They glowed like jewels. Some fish were such a bright blue, they looked like they had light bulbs inside them.

Hundreds of lemon yellow fish shaped like dinner plates fluttered by. They moved

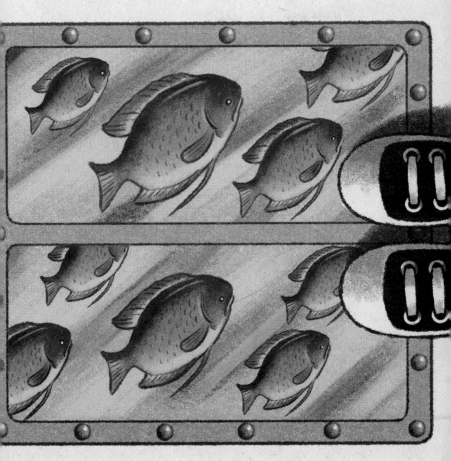

together so perfectly they seemed to be part of one big animal. There were orange fish with purple tiger stripes, green fish speckled with neon blue spots, and fish the color of yellow and orange flames.

Thousands of finger-sized silver fish whirled around and around and made a huge ball shape.

meep . . . "Little fish swim together, look like one big fish," said Thudd. "Try to fool big fish looking for little fish."

"The water is green here," said Andrew. "It was blue when we were near the shore."

meep . . . "Water green cuz lotsa tiny green plants floating here," said Thudd. "Lotsa tiny animals, too. Floating stuff called plankton. Green water mean lotsa plankton. Lotsa food for fish!"

Judy pointed to a fish that looked like it was made from black and orange puzzle pieces. "That's the official state fish of

Hawai'i," she said. "It's called the humu humu nuku nuku apu ah ah!"

Andrew laughed. "I think they picked it because everybody likes to say 'humu humu nuku nuku apu ah ah.'"

Suddenly the big purple button in the middle of Thudd's chest began to blink. It popped open and a beam of purple light zoomed out.

At the end of the beam, a purple hologram of Uncle Al appeared on the dashboard.

"Hey there!" said the Uncle Al hologram. "Where are you guys?"

With his hologram, Uncle Al could hear them but not see them.

"Um, we're in the water," said Andrew.

Uncle Al shook his head. "I know you love the ocean," he said. "But we have to have breakfast and leave for the airport. It's not time for swimming."

"We're not swimming!" said Judy. "We're

trapped in the Water Bug in the middle of the ocean!"

Uncle Al's bushy eyebrows went way up. "Elvis Presley on an English muffin!" he said. "Tell me how this happened!"

Andrew told Uncle Al how he'd been

getting up early to finish the Water Bug.

"Thank you, Andrew," said Uncle Al, "but—"

Andrew interrupted. "And I was just showing it to Judy when the destination dial, um, broke off."

"Good golly, Miss Molly!" said Uncle Al. "The Water Bug must be on autopilot! Where did it say it was going?"

"The deepest ocean," said Andrew.

"How can we get back to the beach?" asked Judy.

"No problem!" said Uncle Al. "As long as the blue wire on the destination dial hasn't broken off. Andrew, do you see the blue wire on the bottom of the dial?"

Andrew picked the dial up off the floor and turned it over. There was no wire at all!

SHARK ATTACK!

"Um, there's no blue wire under the destination dial," said Andrew.

Uncle Al rubbed his chin. "Problems always have more than one solution," he said. "I'll figure out another way to fix the destination dial."

Judy rolled her eyes. "Can't you just use sonar or radar or something to find us?"

"Did you notice the unusual color of the Water Bug?" asked Uncle Al.

"Yup," said Judy. "Andrew said it was some kind of disguise coating."

"It is," said Uncle Al. "The Protectum coating helps to hide the Water Bug from everyone—including me!"

"Bummer!" said Judy. "But why does the Water Bug have to be hidden?"

Uncle Al was quiet for a moment. "Have you guys ever heard of Soggy Bob Sloggins?" he asked.

"Uh-uh," said Andrew.

"Nope," said Judy.

"Soggy Bob Sloggins has been stealing animals from all over the world," said Uncle Al. "Last year, he smuggled a dozen platypuses out of Australia in his suitcases. He packed a pair of pandas out of China in his trunks. The International Police caught him sneaking out of India with a pygmy elephant in a pickup truck."

"Why does he want all those animals?" asked Andrew.

"Soggy Bob is building Animal Universe,"

said Uncle Al, "the biggest theme park ever. But he doesn't care about the animals. He told a reporter that if an animal cost too much to care for, he'd stuff it!"

"Oh no!" said Judy.

"I've been working with the International Police," said Uncle Al. "We've heard that Soggy Bob wants to find and capture giant squids! He's got a huge tank ready. The sign above it says 'Soggy Bob's Giant Squid-wiches—Coming Soon!'"

"We can't let him do it!" said Judy.

"We've got to protect them!" said Andrew.

Uncle Al nodded. "I know how you feel," he said. "I made the Water Bug so I could go anywhere in the ocean and keep Soggy Bob from harming giant squids or—"

Suddenly the Water Bug started to shake! The Uncle Al hologram wiggled like purple Jell-O. Then it disappeared.

"Yikes!" yelled Judy, wobbling in her seat. "Why are we on spin cycle, and what happened to Uncle Al?"

Andrew and Judy peered out the windshield. At first, all they saw was a gray triangle. Then they saw a smooth torpedo shape as long as a car!

"It's a shark!" said Andrew.

The shark had chomped down on the Water Bug's bumper. It was trying to pull it off!

Judy leaned close to the windshield to get a better look. "Why would a shark bite a bumper?" she asked.

Andrew scratched his head. "I made the bumpers out of this special rubber blubber so the Water Bug could bounce off rocks and stuff. But it looks like rubber-blubber buggy bumpers taste good to sharks."

Judy gave Andrew a nasty look.

The shark let go of the bumper and cruised by the windshield.

"Yaaaaah!" yelled Judy. "That's the weird-est head I've ever seen."

The shark's head was as wide as the wind-shield and shaped like the top of the letter *T*. At each end of the *T*, there was a big, dark eye!

meep . . . "Hammerhead shark!" said Thudd. "Sharks use lotsa stuff to find prey. Shark skin feel things move in water. Shark

ears tell if prey animal healthy or sick. Shark nose good smeller. Can feel electricity, too! Electricity come from all things that live. Come from machines! Come from Water Bug!"

The shark's mouth was a curved slit filled with rows and rows of claw-like teeth!

meep . . . "Sharks got three thousand teeth!" said Thudd. "When tooth break off, shark get new one!"

"What's that yucky stuff stuck between its teeth?" asked Judy.

"I think it's little pieces of the rubber-blubber bumper," said Andrew. "That shark could use a toothpick."

Suddenly Andrew saw something in the rearview mirror. More torpedo-shaped creatures! Lots of them! They were twisting and spinning through the water, right toward the Water Bug!

FLOORP!

"Holy moly!" said Andrew. "More sharks!"

"Noop! Noop! Noop!" said Thudd. "Sharks not like to swim with other sharks. Dolphins here!"

"Wowzers!" said Andrew. "It's a whole herd of them!"

meep . . . "Called *pod* of dolphins," said Thudd.

Andrew and Judy turned to get a better look. Most of the dolphins were as big as grown-up humans. But there was one very small dolphin swimming with them.

"It's a dolphin baby!" said Judy.

meep . . . "Dolphin *calf,*" said Thudd.

The shark twisted away from the windshield and started swimming toward the dolphins—right toward the calf!

The Water Bug's outside microphone was picking up strange sounds—clicks and whistles and squawks.

meep . . . "Dolphins talking!" said Thudd.

The big dolphins surrounded the little one. Two of the biggest dolphins broke away from the pod. They charged at the shark! They rammed its belly with their long, beaklike noses.

In a flash, the shark circled behind the two dolphins. The dolphins sped toward the Water Bug. They dove under it. The shark was closing in!

Judy clapped her hand over her mouth. "The shark will get the dolphins," she said. "We've got to do something!"

meep . . . "Press Bug-a-Boo button!" said Thudd, pointing to a red button on the dashboard.

Andrew pressed it.

Floorp! came a sound from outside the Water Bug. Something that looked like a clown's collar popped out from behind the Water Bug's doors. It had red-and-orange stripes and big black spots.

The Bug-a-Boo waggled back and forth furiously in front of the shark's face. It reminded Andrew of a lizard he had seen on a nature show.

"Awesome!" said Andrew.

meep . . . "Bug-a-Boo make Water Bug look big, big, big!" said Thudd. "Make Water Bug look scary!"

The shark stopped and shook its head from side to side. It flipped its tail back and forth like an angry cat. Then it dove deep and disappeared.

Andrew pressed the Bug-a-Boo button again.

Floorp!

The Bug-a-Boo rolled itself back into a groove behind the doors of the Water Bug.

"Whew!" said Andrew, shaking his head.

"At least *something* on the Water Bug is working," said Judy.

The two dolphins swam toward the Water Bug. The bigger one came right up to Judy's window. Its beaky mouth was open.

meep . . . "Dolphin is mammal," said Thudd. "Like Drewd and Oody!"

"It looks like he's laughing!" said Judy.

She patted her hand on the glass. "I love dolphins. They're really smart. Maybe he understands that I'm saying hi."

"Look at his tail," said Andrew. "It looks like something took a bite out of it."

Thudd waved at the dolphin.

meep . . . "Hiya, Nahu!" Thudd squeaked.

"Why did you call him Nahu?" asked Judy.

meep . . . "*Nahu* is Hawaiian word for 'bite,'" said Thudd.

The dolphins were making whistling sounds.

meep . . . "See hole at top of dolphin

37

head?" said Thudd. "Called blowhole. Dolphin use blowhole to breathe. Dolphin use blowhole to make sounds. To talk. Dolphin talk got lotsa clicks and whistles. Every dolphin got own special whistle. Like name for human."

The dolphins followed the Water Bug as it went deeper.

The dial on the dashboard said they were fifty feet deep now.

Suddenly Andrew glimpsed something strange through the Water Bug's glass floor.

"Wowzers!" said Andrew, pointing below them. "It looks like a stony gray castle surrounded by a field of blue moose antlers!"

Judy's eyes got wide. "Maybe it's Atlantis!" she said.

Andrew's mouth dropped open. "I see a giant brain!"

TWINKLE, TWINKLE, LITTLE STARFISH

meep . . . "Not Atlantis! Not brain!" said Thudd. "Coral. Strange shapes made by lotsa tiny coral animals."

Thudd flashed a picture of a coral animal on his screen.

meep . . . "Coral animal got skeleton on outside. Skeleton like little house. When old coral animal die, skeleton stay. Baby coral animal build new skeleton on top of old skeletons. Millions, millions coral skeletons stick together. Pile up! Make coral mountain. Can make whole island!"

The Water Bug paddled over coral that looked like pink cauliflower and skinny green fingers and giant mushrooms.

Fish darted in and out among the nooks and crannies of the coral. Some stopped to nibble seaweed.

The Water Bug was near a mound of coral that looked like a pile of dirty snow. Crawling over it were bright red star-shaped animals as big as platters. They had lots of arms and were covered with thorny spines.

"Scary-looking starfish!" said Judy.

meep . . . "Not fish," said Thudd. "Better name for starfish is sea star. Scary for coral. Eat lotsa coral animals."

"Watch this!" Andrew said. He pressed a black button on the dashboard and the Water Bug's hood popped open. Out wriggled eight long tentacles. They were gray with black speckles and covered with round suckers.

"It's the Octo-Tool," said Andrew. He leaned toward the microphone on the dashboard. "Remove sea stars!" he ordered.

The tentacles reached out, plucked the sea stars off the coral, and plopped them down in the sand.

Andrew turned to Judy. "See?" he said.

The tentacles of the Octo-Tool froze.

glurp . . . "You want to *see* the sea stars?" asked the Water Bug. "It is not a good idea, but if that is what you want . . ."

"*Noooooo!*" said Andrew.

It was too late. Octo-Tool tentacles were pushing in through a rubber door under the steering wheel. Each tentacle was holding a huge wriggling sea star!

meep . . . "Got poison spines!" said Thudd.

"Yiiiiikes!" yelled Judy. She ducked as a sea star whizzed over her head.

Andrew grabbed a tentacle of the Octo-Tool. Then he caught another and another.

He pushed them back through the door under the steering wheel.

"Out!" he yelled. "Take the sea stars *out!"*

glurp . . . "Make up your mind, please," said the Water Bug.

Andrew and Judy snatched the last two Octo-Tool tentacles and shoved them through the door.

"Whew!" said Andrew, wiping his hands on his pants.

"Disgusting!" said Judy, pushing her hair away from her face.

They leaned back in their seats—just in time to watch the Water Bug slide into the mouth of a stony underwater cave!

It was dark as midnight inside.

meep . . . "'Fraid of dark!" said Thudd.

Andrew pulled a knob on the dashboard, and the Water Bug's headlights snapped on.

"Thunkoo!" said Thudd.

The walls of the cave were splotched with

bright lumps—red and green and orange and pink and yellow.

"Look at those colors!" said Judy. "It looks like some little kid glopped finger paint everywhere!"

meep . . . "Sponges!" said Thudd. "Sponge animals like to live on walls of underwater cave."

A lot of strange animals seemed to like the cave. Creatures shaped like feathery black fans dangled from the ceiling and swayed in the water. A family of lobsters with blue tails scuttled between the rocks.

Judy pointed to a small spotted fish in front of the windshield. "What beautiful blue eyes it has!" she said.

Suddenly the fish blew up to the size of a basketball! There were spines all over it!

UH-OH!

meep . . . "Porcupine fish!" said Thudd.
"When porcupine fish afraid, blow itself up!
Spines pop up. Other fish not swallow it!"

The porcupine fish batted its fins angrily. But when it couldn't make the Water Bug go away, it took off into the gloom.

The cave was crawling with strange sights. Blue sausage-shaped creatures with black stripes slithered over the rocks. One rock was crowded with black pincushion-shaped animals covered with needles as long as knives.

A red skirt-like creature twirled in front of the windshield like a ballerina.

meep . . . "Spanish dancer sea slug," said Thudd. "Like big snail without shell."

A dark wall of the cave twinkled with light. As the Water Bug got closer, Andrew and Judy saw clam-like creatures clinging to the rocks. Their shells were open. Inside, flashes of light flickered.

"Wowzers!" said Andrew. "It looks like tiny lightning inside those shells!"

meep . . . "Flame scallop animal!" said

Thudd. "Make light inside! Lotsa sea creatures make light. Called bioluminescence. Means 'light made by living thing.'"

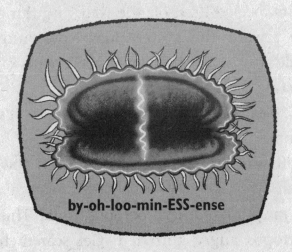

by-oh-loo-min-ESS-ense

Andrew squinted at a rock next to the flame scallops.

"I think that rock has *eyes*!" he said.

meep . . . "Stonefish!" said Thudd. "Look like rock. Not move. Wait for prey animal. Stonefish got big poison in skin! Human step on stonefish, can die!"

The headlights of the Water Bug fell on a

bumpy pink lump smooshed into a corner. It looked like a humongous glob of Silly Putty!

In the next instant, the glob turned white, peeled itself off the wall, and flung itself toward the Water Bug! Now Andrew could see it was balloon-shaped, with eight twisting tentacles at the bottom.

"Neato mosquito!" yelled Andrew. "It's an octopus!"

It was turning red as it zoomed toward them.

meep . . . "Angry octopus," said Thudd. "Octopus angry, turn red. Get scared, turn white."

The octopus slapped itself onto the hood of the Water Bug. It poked one of its tentacles inside the Super-Sniffer!

"It's trying to pick the Super-Sniffer's nose!" said Andrew.

meep . . . "Octopus looking for clams," said Thudd.

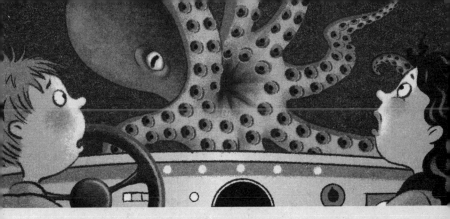

Andrew pressed a button on the dashboard. The Super-Sniffer twitched. The octopus seemed startled and pulled its tentacle out
of the Super-Sniffer. Then it crawled up to the
windshield. It gripped the glass with its round
suckers and looked in at Andrew and Judy.

"Weirdo eyes!" said Judy.

The pupils of the octopus's eyes weren't
round like a human's. They were narrow
black slits.

The octopus was changing color again.
Pink and blue and purple began to flicker
across its skin like a neon sign!

meep . . . "Octopus excited to see us!" said
Thudd.

The octopus slapped its tentacles against the window on Judy's side. It looked like it was tugging!

"I think it wants to get in," said Judy. "It's actually kind of cute, in a weird way."

The octopus gave up and jetted back to the cave wall. It slithered over to a patch of bumpy purple sponges. In a moment, its color matched the sponges. Its skin became just as bumpy.

meep . . . "Octopus change skin to hide," said Thudd. "Octopus eyes connect to octopus skin. Make octopus skin match what octopus see!"

Suddenly the octopus turned white and puffed out a smoky black cloud! The water in front of the Water Bug turned dark as mud.

meep . . . "Octopus make black ink," said Thudd. "Hide from enemy!"

"What's scaring it?" asked Andrew.

CLACK! CLACK! CLACK! came a noise.

The whole Water Bug was shaking!

CLACK! CLACK! CLACK!

Beams of blinding orange light cut through the cloud of octopus ink.

Coming toward the Water Bug was a

giant metal crab! The top of it was a glass dome.

CLACK! CLACK! CLACK!

Its two monster claws were snapping.

"Holy moly!" said Andrew. "What's that?"

meep . . . "Crab-Mobile!" said Thudd. "Soggy Bob inside!"

"Cheese Louise!" said Judy. Her eyes were as round as gumballs.

A small door at the front of the shiny metal crab slid open. A black thing as thick as a fire hose and as long as a car slithered out.

It speedily snaked its way to the Water Bug and swam in a circle around it. The Water Bug stopped moving. Yellow sparks were popping off its hood and doors.

Zitt zitt zitt!

The Water Bug was sizzling!

8 GETTING CRABBY

Thudd pulled himself out of Andrew's pocket. With his little rubbery, jellybean-shaped feet, he climbed up to Andrew's shoulder.

meep . . . "New kind of giant electric eel!" said Thudd.

Andrew pressed the Octo-Tool button. "Catch eel!" he yelled.

The Water Bug's hood sprang open. The Octo-Tool flung its tentacles at the eel! They missed. The eel was too fast.

Then the tentacles stopped moving. They stayed very still. The eel stopped circling the

Water Bug. It went over to the Octo-Tool and opened its mouth wide. It was about to chomp down on a juicy tentacle!

The Octo-Tool sprang into action. The tentacles latched on to the eel, spun it around, and sent it zooming back toward the Crab-Mobile. The Water Bug stopped sizzling.

The metal crab crept closer. The dome lit up with a greenish glow.

Inside the dome, Andrew and Judy could see a man with a curly black mustache and a head as bald as a light bulb. The muscles of his arms bulged under his T-shirt like grapefruits. He sat in a big chair covered in zebra stripes.

Perched on the back of the chair was an enormous blue parrot.

meep . . . "Soggy Bob got Burpp with him," said Thudd. "'Burpp' short for **Bob's Ultra-Robot Parrot Partner.**"

Soggy Bob pushed his face close to the

glass dome of the Crab-Mobile.

Kkk . . . kkkkk . . . kkkkkkk crackled the speaker on the dashboard. "Well, lookee here, Burpp," came the growly voice of Soggy Bob Sloggins. He poked Burpp on his wing. "A surprise!

"Heh! Heh! Heh!" laughed Soggy Bob. "Ah was expectin' that shaggy-haired, fuzzy-brained Professor Dubble feller! But it's just two skinny kids! Hi, kiddies! Thanks to my eel buddy, ah can talk to ya whenever ah want to!"

Andrew pushed out his chin like he

always did when he was trying not to look afraid. Judy just folded her arms and frowned.

Soggy Bob laughed. "Ya look scared as mice in a litter box! No chance of ya babies findin' them there giant squids!"

Awwwwwk! Burpp flapped his wings. "You betcha, boss!" squawked Burpp. "Nobody knows the ocean like we do."

Soggy Bob frowned. "But let's make real sure ya little critters won't do nothin' that messes up my plan," he said.

Clack! Clack! Clack!

"And don't bother screamin'," said Soggy Bob, "cuz ah can't hear ya. This conversation is one-way only! Heh! Heh! Heh!"

The Crab-Mobile snapped its huge steel claws. It began to creep closer and closer to the Water Bug.

"Oh no!" said Judy. "What can we do?"

"Not much," said Andrew, "since we can't steer the Water Bug."

Judy touched her lip with her tongue. "I have an idea," she said.

Judy picked the destination dial up off the floor. She pulled a hairpin from her long frizzy hair and straightened it out. She poked one end of the hairpin through the bottom of the destination dial. She poked the other end of the hairpin into the hole in the dashboard where the dial had been. She gave the destination dial a twist.

"Now try the steering wheel," said Judy.

Andrew turned the steering wheel. The Water Bug turned, too!

"Way to go, Judy!" Andrew cheered.

He pushed the Octo-Tool button. "Start Escape Jet!" he yelled.

A fat black tube popped out from under the hood of the Water Bug.

"What's that goofy thing?" asked Judy.

meep . . . "To escape, Water Bug move like octopus," said Thudd. "Suck in water through tube. Then push water out fast, fast, fast! Like garden hose!"

Andrew pulled the steering wheel up,

looked in the rearview mirror, and slammed his foot on the gas pedal. The Water Bug jiggled. Then . . .

Slooooosh!

The Water Bug shot backward like an underwater spitball! It jetted away from the Crab-Mobile!

"Super-duper pooper scooper!" yelled Andrew. He steered the Water Bug out of the dark cave and into the green water.

"Start Ink Jet!" Andrew yelled.

The black tube squirted a big blob of black ink into the water.

"That should keep Soggy Bob off our trail for a while," said Andrew.

He shut off the Escape Jet and spun the Water Bug around. There was nothing but fish behind them. After a few minutes, Andrew slowed down.

"Whew!" said Andrew. "We got away! The Crab-Mobile is a lot slower than the Water Bug."

Judy turned to Andrew. "You know," she said, "now that we can steer the Water Bug, we could get back to shore."

"Yup," said Andrew. "But we can't go back until we stop Soggy Bob."

"I hate to say it," said Judy, "but for the first time in your bug-brain life, maybe you're right."

Just then, Thudd's purple button started to blink. In a second, a purple Uncle Al hologram was perched on the dashboard.

SQUIDS AHOY!

Uncle Al's hologram was more transparent than before.

"Hey there, guys!" he said. His voice sounded far away.

"Hi, Uncle Al," said Andrew.

"Hiya, Unkie!" said Thudd.

"It's hard to hear you, Uncle Al," said Judy.

"The Hologram Helper has problems underwater," said Uncle Al. "But the good news is that I've figured out a way to fix the destination dial. Judy, do you have a hairpin?"

"Yes!" said Judy. "And I fixed it already!"

"And we met Soggy Bob in an underwater cave," said Andrew, "and we escaped!"

"King Arthur on a Girl Scout cookie!" said Uncle Al. "You guys are amazing! Now we can get the three of you back!"

"But by the time we get back," said Andrew, "it may be too late to save the squids!"

"Yes!" agreed Judy. "We can't let Soggy Bob turn them into squidwiches!"

Uncle Al shook his head. "You guys are very brave," he said. "But I can't let you take on Soggy Bob by yourselves. You're much more important than squids!"

"We got away from Soggy Bob once," said Andrew. "We can do it again."

Uncle Al looked very serious. "I'm worried about more than just Soggy Bob," he said. "The deep ocean is the most dangerous place on earth!" His voice was getting softer.

meep . . . "At deepest ocean, seven miles of water above!" said Thudd. "Water heavy as herd of elephants!"

"But, Uncle Al," said Andrew, "I thought the Water Bug's coating of Protectum would keep it from getting squashed."

"But there are other things, too," said Uncle Al. "There are sea creatures that are hard to imagine."

Andrew's eyes got wide. "I *like* to imagine things that are hard to imagine," he said.

"Well," said Uncle Al. His voice was fading, and so was his hologram. "It's not only the animals that are alive down there. The earth is alive, too! You may get to see how alive it really is. I don't want you to . . ."

"We can't hear you, Uncle Al!" said Judy.

All that was left of Uncle Al were his bushy eyebrows floating above the dashboard. Then they disappeared, too.

"Super-bummer!" said Judy. "So what's

this big deal about the earth being alive?"

meep . . . "Earth changing all the time,"
said Thudd. "Like living thing. This what
earth look like two hundred million years
ago."

Thudd's face screen showed one giant
continent surrounded by water.

"Wowzers schnauzers!" said Andrew. "What happened?"

meep . . . "Earth kinda like big pie," said Thudd. "Outside of earth called crust. Earth crust broken. Lotsa pieces. Underneath crust, earth got layer of melted rock. Hot, hot, hot! Earth crust float on melted rock, like crust on top of pie."

Judy shook her head. "I thought the earth was like a giant rock," she said, "with a blanket of dirt on top for plants."

"Noop!" said Thudd. "Earth crust break up. Pieces move. Millions, millions years ago, South America stuck to Africa!"

"You mean the continents moved thousands of miles?" asked Judy.

"Yoop!" said Thudd. "Pieces of earth crust always moving. Move as fast as fingernail grow. North America moving away from Europe. Getting closer to Japan!"

"Sounds goofy," said Judy. She leaned

over to Thudd. "Did your brain chips get soggy again, little guy?" she asked.

"Noop! Noop! Noop!" said Thudd.

Judy looked at her fingers. "Who cares if continents are moving around as fast as fingernails grow," she said. "That's not going to bother us."

She looked at Andrew. "I say we go find some giant squids!"

"Neato mosquito!" said Andrew. "I'll turn on the Super-Sniffer." Andrew pressed a silver button on the dashboard.

"Search for giant squids!" said Andrew into the microphone.

glurp . . . "I was hoping you would say that!" said the Water Bug.

A compass lit up in the middle of the steering wheel. The words "giant squid" lit up in green letters at the top.

glurp . . . "When the arrow points to 'giant squid,' you are going in the right—"

Booooooooooom! came a huge sound from below. It sounded like someone banging on an enormous drum!

Boooooom! Boooooom!

Andrew and Judy looked at each other.

"What's that?" asked Judy.

"Could it be Soggy Bob?" asked Andrew.

"Noop! Noop! Noop!" squeaked Thudd. "Earthquake! Earth crust cracking! Earth crust moving!"

Suddenly the water lit up with a glow as red as a monster barbecue grill!

Through the glass floor of the Water Bug, Andrew and Judy could see a dark underwater mountain. The top of it was on fire! Stuff that looked like orange-red cake batter was pouring down the sides!

"Wowzers schnauzers!" Andrew said. "It looks like the volcano we flew over in Hawai'i!"

meep . . . "Underwater volcano!" said

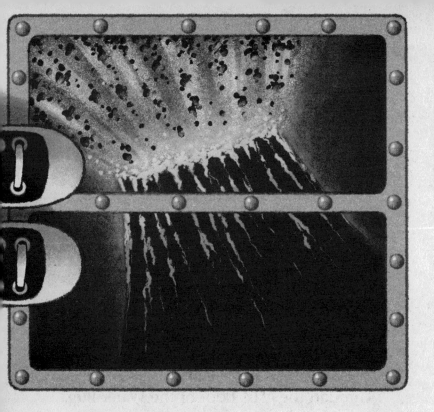

Thudd. "Melted rock called lava come up from inside earth. Spill out! Lava hot, hot, hot! Two thousand degrees! If stuff fall into volcano, stuff not burn. Stuff turn to dust! Disappear!"

"We'd better get out of here," said Andrew.

"Fast!" said Judy.

A BAD TIME FOR BOOGERS . . .

Andrew slammed his foot down on the gas pedal. The Water Bug shot off.

meep . . . "Baby Hawaiian island getting born here! All Hawaiian islands born from volcanoes," said Thudd. "Hot lava pour out on bottom of ocean. When lava get cool, turn into rock. Lotsa, lotsa rock pile up. Make island! Baby island take lotsa years to grow up. Maybe in ten thousand years, humans visit new island!"

Pillow-shaped chunks of lava rocketed up toward the Water Bug. *Clunk! Cachunk!*

Lava rocks were crashing into the glass floor of the Water Bug and bouncing off the hood!

Orange fireworks exploded around the Water Bug. Andrew couldn't tell if he was going toward the volcano or away from it!

Then something strange started happening.

Bop! Bop! Bop!

The Water Bug was being pushed into calmer water. Someone was helping them!

The bumping and pushing didn't stop until the Water Bug was away from the fountains of fire.

Dark shadows shot up through the water. One of the shadows had a bite in its tail.

"It's Nahu and his friend!" said Judy.

The two dolphins tapped their noses on the windshield.

"They pushed us away from the volcano!" said Andrew.

"We love you!" said Judy, patting the windshield.

The dolphins looked like they were smiling! Clicks and whistles came through the speaker.

Suddenly the compass in the middle of the steering wheel started blinking red. The compass needle was spinning around and around.

"Uh-oh," said Andrew. "Something's wrong with the Super-Sniffer."

glurp . . . "The Super-Sniffer has lava boogers!" said the Water Bug.

Andrew peered out at the hood. The Super-Sniffer was twitching.

glurp . . . "Cannot find the trail of the giant squid until boogers are removed."

"This should be easy," said Andrew. He pressed the Octo-Tool button. "Remove boogers from the Super-Sniffer!" he commanded.

The hood popped up, and tentacles slithered out.

Two of the tentacles poked up into the Super-Sniffer's nostrils. They twisted around inside for a long time.

glurp . . . "Octo-Tool tentacles are stuck inside the Super-Sniffer," said the Water Bug. "Must remove tentacles. Must use the Nose Pick to remove boogers."

"Nose Pick!" said Judy. "Yuck-a-rama!"

"I think it's in the toolbox," said Andrew.

Andrew crept between the seats to the tiny kitchen at the back of the Water Bug.

He opened the cabinet under the sink and took out a metal toolbox.

Inside the box were hammers and pliers and wrenches and screwdrivers. And there was a big fuzzy finger with a handle.

"The Nose Pick!" said Andrew, pulling the fuzzy finger out of the box.

"What are you going to do with that

stupid thing?" Judy asked. "You can't go outside."

"Just a minute," said Andrew, ducking back under the sink. When he came out, he was holding two football-sized green blobs covered with bumps.

Andrew handed one of the blobs to Judy.

"We *can* go outside," said Andrew. "Just pull on these Bubble Duds over your clothes. They'll keep you dry and warm and let you breathe.

"Look," said Andrew, pointing to the bumps on the green blob. "These are bubbles with air inside. And they can pull more oxygen from the water."

Judy touched the blob. It was sticky and squishy.

"You've *got* to be kidding," said Judy.

"Um, no," said Andrew. "I need you to come outside and hold the flashlight so I can see the lava boogers and pull them out."

Andrew unsnapped the mini-flashlight he always carried on his belt loop and handed it to Judy.

"Cheese Louise!" said Judy. "Remind me to never, ever, *ever* let you talk me into anything ever again!"

Andrew went back to the front seat. He slipped Thudd into a little plastic sack called the Bubble Bag. The Bubble Bag would keep Thudd dry. Thudd was never supposed to get wet!

Then Andrew took his blob and began to stretch it over his feet. He pulled it up to his waist, stretched it over his arms, and tugged it up to his neck.

The Bubble Duds had pockets all over them. Andrew tucked Thudd into a little pocket over his chest and pressed the pocket closed. He put the Nose Pick into another pocket.

Judy laughed. "You look like a big green frog," she said.

"Come on, Judy," said Andrew. "Put on the Bubble Duds. Please."

"Oh, all right," said Judy. She pulled the blob of Bubble Duds up over her clothes. "So how do we get out of here?"

"Just press the button on the side of your seat," said Andrew. "Watch this!" He pulled the Bubble Duds over his head. Then he pressed the button on the side of his seat.

FLAMP!

The seat flipped over!

In an instant, Andrew was outside the Water Bug. The water was swarming with a zillion tiny shrimp-like creatures. Andrew brushed them away and tapped on Judy's window. "Hurry up!" he said into the little microphone inside the Bubble Duds.

Judy made a grumpy face, but her seat flipped over, and the next second she was in the water next to Andrew.

Andrew and Judy swam toward the Super-Sniffer. Andrew pulled the Octo-Tool tentacle out of the Super-Sniffer's nose. He was reaching for the Nose Pick when . . .

MoooOOOOOoooOOOOaaahhh! came the strangest sound Andrew had ever heard. He could actually *feel* it!

It sounds like a million-pound cow! thought Andrew.

Andrew and Judy turned. Something huge and dark was coming up behind them. It was shaped like the bottom of an enormous ship!

Could that be a submarine? thought Andrew. *Uh-oh, submarines don't have humongous mouths with tongues the size of elephants! Unless I can think of something fast, we're going to be a monster's dinner!*

TO BE CONTINUED IN ANDREW, JUDY, AND THUDD'S NEXT EXCITING ADVENTURE!

ANDREW LOST IN THE WHALE!

In stores October 2003

TRUE STUFF

Thudd wanted to say more about Hawai'i and the ocean, but Andrew and Judy were busy with sea stars, volcanoes, and Soggy Bob. Here's what Thudd wanted to say:

• You probably see the name of the fiftieth state spelled *Hawaii*. But in the language of the Hawaiian people, it's spelled with an apostrophe: *Hawai'i*. So that's the way we spell it in this book. Interestingly, the word *Hawaiian* is spelled without an apostrophe.

• The Hawaiian language uses only twelve letters! They are A, E, I, O, U, H, K, L, M, N, P, W.

• Have you ever seen a school of fish turn at

exactly the same moment? All fish have thin lines along the sides of their bodies. Inside these lines are little hairs that feel the tiniest changes in the movement of the water. As each fish moves, the other fish feel it and instantly move the same way.

• Humans breathe automatically. Whether we're awake or asleep, our brains keep us breathing. Dolphins breathe voluntarily. That means they have to *choose* to breathe, the way we choose to move an arm or a leg. To keep breathing, dolphins can never be completely asleep. Half of a dolphin's brain sleeps while the other half stays awake!

• Want to see the air that's in water? Look at an ice cube. Do you see the white stuff at the center of the cube? That white stuff is lots of little air bubbles. When water freezes, the air is squeezed out and trapped in those bubbles.

• Corals have many beautiful colors. All those colors come from algae (AL-jee), which are like tiny plants. Algae live inside the coral animals and make food for them. The coral provides a home for the algae. Everybody wins! Living together in this way is called symbiosis (sim-bee-OH-sis).

• When an octopus is attacked, it can detach a tentacle. The tentacle keeps on wriggling— hopefully the predator will chase the tentacle instead of the octopus! In a few weeks, the octopus will grow a new tentacle. When some sea stars lose their arms, the arm can grow into a brand-new sea star!

• If all the salt in all the oceans were piled up on land, every inch of the earth would be buried under 500 feet of salt. That's about as tall as a fifty-story office building! Where does all this salt come from? Rivers constantly wash salt out of the soil and into the oceans. Rivers wash many other minerals out of the rocks and soil, too.

WHERE TO FIND MORE TRUE STUFF

Want to find out about the amazing and mysterious things that can happen in the underwater world? Read these books!

• *Dolphin Adventure* by Wayne Grover (New York: HarperTrophy, 1990). This is the true story of how a family of dolphins asked humans for help to save their injured baby!

• *Shark Lady: True Adventures of Eugenie Clark* by Ann McGovern (New York: Scholastic, 1978) and *Adventures of the Shark Lady: Eugenie Clark Around the World* by Ann McGovern (New York: Scholastic, 1998). In these books, a nine-year-old girl who loves to watch the fish in her aquarium grows up to study sea creatures all over the world. She swims with flashlight fish, rides a monster whale shark, and gets caught in the claws of a giant spider crab!

• *Eyewitness: Ocean* by Miranda Macquitty (New York: DK Publishing, 2000). Lots of information and great pictures tell the story of the oceans—how they were made, what lives in them, and how we explore them.

• *The Octopus: Phantom of the Sea* by Mary M. Cerullo (New York: Cobblehill Books/Dutton, 1997). Want to find out more about smart octopuses, including the tricks they play on humans? Read this!

• *Hidden Hawaii,* a video created and directed by Robert Hillman (Ogden, UT: Destination Cinema, 2000). Would you like to take a quick trip to Hawai'i without getting on a plane? Find this video! You'll see volcanoes, including the underwater volcano named Loihi, coral reefs, and some very strange plants.

Turn the page
for a sneak peek at
Andrew, Judy, and Thudd's
brand-new adventure—

ANDREW LOST
IN THE WHALE!

Available October 2003

A WHALE OF A PROBLEM

"YOWZERS!" yelled Andrew as he floated under the shadowy green water. His eyes bugged out. Something that looked like a blue-gray submarine was swimming toward him and his cousin Judy. Its mouth was as big as a garage!

Swarms of pink shrimp creatures swirled around them. The monster mouth swooped closer.

"Cheese Louise!" yelled Judy. "It's coming right at us!"

Her eyes were wide behind the face mask of her Bubble Duds underwater suit.

meep . . . "Blue whale!" came a squeaky voice from a pocket of Andrew's Bubble Duds. It was Andrew's little silver robot friend, Thudd.

meep . . . "Blue whale big, big, big!" said Thudd. "Big as six brontosaurs! Big as twenty-five elephants! Long as three school buses!"

Oooooooaaaaaaaaaaaauuu! came a huge sound through the special headphones in the helmet of Andrew's Bubble Duds. The Bubble Duds headphones picked up every sound, even some that humans couldn't usually hear.

Andrew could feel the sound, too. It shook him from his head to his toes.

Judy dove under the Water Bug. The Water Bug was an underwater vehicle made from an old Volkswagen Beetle.

"Andrew!" yelled Judy. "Get back into the Water Bug right now. That whale is going to *eat* us!"

meep . . . "Drewd and Oody too big for blue whale to eat," said Thudd. "Blue whale eat tiny shrimpy stuff."

Thudd pointed to the little pink creatures all around them. "Called krill," said Thudd.

Andrew dove under the Water Bug. He tried to find the button to get them back inside. But the gigantic mouth and its blubbery lips were just inches away!

"Noooo!" yelled Judy.

"Holy moly!" yelled Andrew.

"Noooop!" squeaked Thudd.

The mouth swooshed up a swimming pool–sized gulp of water—and Andrew, Judy, Thudd, and the Water Bug with it!

A STEPPING STONE BOOK™

Great stories by great authors . . .
for fantastic first reading experiences!

Grades 1–3

FICTION

Duz Shedd series
by Marjorie Weinman Sharmat
Junie B. Jones series by Barbara Park
Magic Tree House® series
by Mary Pope Osborne
Marvin Redpost series by Louis Sachar
Mole and Shrew books
by Jackie French Koller
Tooter Tales books by Jerry Spinelli

The Chalk Box Kid
by Clyde Robert Bulla
The Paint Brush Kid
by Clyde Robert Bulla
White Bird by Clyde Robert Bulla

NONFICTION

Magic Tree House® Research Guide
by Will Osborne and
Mary Pope Osborne

Grades 2–4

A to Z Mysteries® series by Ron Roy
Aliens for . . . books
by Stephanie Spinner & Jonathan Etra
Julian books by Ann Cameron
The Katie Lynn Cookie Company series
by G. E. Stanley
The Case of the Elevator Duck
by Polly Berrien Berends
Hannah by Gloria Whelan
Little Swan by Adèle Geras
The Minstrel in the Tower
by Gloria Skurzynski

Next Spring an Oriole
by Gloria Whelan
Night of the Full Moon
by Gloria Whelan
Silver by Gloria Whelan
Smasher by Dick King-Smith

CLASSICS

Dr. Jekyll and Mr. Hyde
retold by Stephanie Spinner
Dracula retold by Stephanie Spinner
Frankenstein retold by Larry Weinberg

Grades 3–5

FICTION

The Magic Elements Quartet
by Mallory Loehr
Spider Kane Mysteries
by Mary Pope Osborne

NONFICTION

Balto and the Great Race
by Elizabeth Cody Kimmel
The *Titanic* Sinks!
by Thomas Conklin